W9-BZC-058

For Every Dog An Angel

written and illustrated by
Christine Davis

For Every Dog An Angel

Printed in Hong Kong

Lighthearted Press Inc.
P.O. Box 90125
Portland, OR 97290

ISBN 0-9659225-0-2
10 9 8 7 6 5

Acknowledgements

*With gratitude and love I would like to thank
the many dogs who have walked by my side
and shared their dog magic with me.*

*To my loving guides Grandfather, Ione and
Adama—thank you for entrusting this story
to me. May we meet again, soon, to talk
about cats.*

*Most of all, thank you to my husband,
Michael, with whom I share this wondrous
journey—I love you.*

For Martha,
my forever dog,
whose
gentle spirit
and
magic heart
light the
pages of this
book.

Whenever a puppy is born on earth, a guardian angel waits nearby to welcome the puppy into the world and take it under her heavenly wings.

The guardian angel makes herself very small and snuggles in close to the soft, warm fur, telling her puppy how much it is loved and that it has come into the world for a special purpose. Even though the puppy's eyes are closed, it feels the fluttering wings by its heart and knows its guardian angel is there.

All puppies come into the world with unique gifts. As time passes and the puppy grows, the guardian angel helps her puppy to understand what makes it so very special. Whether they are destined to become

fast runners,

soulful singers

or

peaceful sleepers,

each puppy is perfect and the angel loves it just the way it is.

The day comes when the puppy must go into the world and start traveling down its own special path.

Sometimes that path leads to a loving home, where a family is waiting to take their new four-legged friend into their hearts. And the guardian angel is happy, knowing her dog will always have friends to play with, bones to chew on and someone to cuddle up next to at night.

Angels like to visit when their dogs are dreaming. You may have seen a dog's paws moving while it is asleep. Perhaps it is on a high hill in a faraway place, dancing with its guardian angel.

All dogs bring the gift of love to the world. In that way they are very much like angels. Dogs will share their love with anyone. They don't ask for anything in return. But if someone takes a moment to scratch a dog under its chin or tell a dog how special it is, you can be sure its guardian angel is smiling.

From time to time, when a certain person and a certain dog meet, something happens that is just like magic! It is as if they have known each other before. Each knows what the other is thinking and feeling. They will be together always. And the guardian angel watches over the two with love, knowing their dog has found its forever person and the person has found its forever dog.

Forever

A forever person and their forever dog will share many experiences over a lifetime

like listening to favorite stories

and

taking vacations together.

Mountain Cabins Next Left

They will watch hundreds of sunsets from up on the hill.

But the greatest gift these friends will share is knowing what is in the other's heart. Side by side, looking up at the sky on a starry night, a forever person and their forever dog will share all the secret hopes and dreams that are only told to a very best friend.

A dog can never really be separated from its forever person. Neither time nor space can ever come between them. So when the dog comes to the end of its earthly life, and must go on ahead without its person beside them, the guardian angel becomes a loving bridge that connects the two friends for as long as the person remains on earth.

S ometimes dogs will cross the angel bridge and visit the earth while they are waiting for their forever person to join them. You can never be certain where they might turn up.

Y ou may feel four paws padding along next to you when you are walking in the park.

Listen carefully, and you might hear a familiar voice joining in when you go holiday caroling.

So if you see the blanket rumple softly after you've curled up for an afternoon nap, it's very possible your forever dog has come back to visit and is napping beside you.

Nothing brings your forever dog more joy than knowing you are happy, even if that means bringing a new dog companion into your life. Your forever dog lovingly remembers the special place it had in your life on earth, and is delighted to know another dog will get to share all the love you have to offer.

Animal Shelter

Your forever dog may even come back and help your new dog discover the best spots for burying bones

and

show them where to watch for your return at the end of the day.

So don't be surprised to
see your new dog racing
through the house as if
it's playing with an
invisible friend...
it probably is.

As the years go by you and your dog may find yourselves going more slowly as you take your daily walks. The time may come when your dog leaves your side and crosses the bridge to be with your forever dog. In fact, there may be many animals who will share your life during the time you are here on earth.

One day, the angel bridge that your forever dog crossed so many years earlier will appear to you. And with the happy heart of a person who is going home, you will cross the bridge and find yourself welcomed by all the animal friends you made when you were on earth.

In the middle of all that love, your forever dog will be waiting for you. It will be like the day you found each other on earth. You will know you have been together before, and nothing will ever separate you again.

And the angels will be happy, knowing a forever person and their forever dog have found each other once more.

We hope you enjoyed this Lighthearted Press book.
To order additional copies please call our toll free
order number 1-87PETLOVER (1-877-385-6837) or
send $9.95 per copy plus $4.00 shipping per order to:

Lighthearted Press Inc.
P.O. Box 90125
Portland, Oregon 97290
503-786-3085 (Phone)
503-786-0315 (Fax)
1-87PETLOVER (Toll-free)
davis@lightheartedpress.com
www.lightheartedpress.com

Also by Christine Davis
FOR EVERY CAT AN ANGEL